APPLEY DAPPLY'S
NURSERY RHYMES

APPLEY DAPPLY'S
NURSERY RHYMES

BY

BEATRIX POTTER

Author of
" The Tale of Peter Rabbit," etc.

LONDON
FREDERICK WARNE & CO., Ltd.
AND NEW YORK

ISBN 0 7232 0613 9

PRINTED IN GREAT BRITAIN FOR THE PUBLISHERS
BY HENRY STONE AND SON (PRINTERS) LTD., BANBURY
D.6308.880

APPLEY DAPPLY, a little
brown mouse,
Goes to the cupboard in somebody's house.

IN somebody's cupboard
    There's everything nice,
Cake, cheese, jam, biscuits,
    —All charming for mice !

APPLEY DAPPLY has little
    sharp eyes,
And Appley Dapply is *so* fond
    of pies !

NOW who is this knocking
    at Cottontail's door ?
Tap tappit !   Tap tappit !
    She's heard it before ?

15

AND when she peeps out
there is nobody there,
But a present of carrots
put down on the stair.

HARK ! I hear it again !
    Tap, tap, tappit ! Tap
        tappit !
Why—I really believe it's a
        little black rabbit !

19

OLD Mr. Pricklepin
has never a cushion to
stick his pins in,
His nose is black and his
beard is gray,
And he lives in an ash stump
over the way.

YOU know the old woman
who lived in a shoe?
And had so many children
She didn't know what to
do?

I THINK if she lived in
a little shoe-house—
That little old woman was
surely a mouse !

DIGGORY DIGGORY
DELVET !
A little old man in black
velvet ;
He digs and he delves—
You can see for yourselves
The mounds dug by Diggory
Delvet.

GRAVY and potatoes
  In a good brown pot—
Put them in the oven,
  and serve them very hot !

THERE once was an amiable
    guinea-pig,
Who brushed back his hair like
    a periwig—

HE wore a sweet tie,
　As blue as the sky—

34

A ND his whiskers and
buttons
Were very big.

Printed for the Publishers by
Henry Stone & Son (Printers) Ltd., Banbury

1768·1177

The "PETER RABBIT" BOOKS
by BEATRIX POTTER.